OWW!

For Elsie
M.R.

For Joseph
J.L.

First published in hardback in Great Britain by HarperCollins*Publishers* Ltd in 2003
First published in paperback by HarperCollins *Children's Books* in 2004
This edition published in 2022

HarperCollins *Children's Books* is a division of HarperCollins*Publishers* Ltd
1 London Bridge Street, London SE1 9GF

www.harpercollins.co.uk

HarperCollins*Publishers*
1st Floor, Watermarque Building, Ringsend Road, Dublin 4, Ireland

5 7 9 10 8 6

Text copyright © Michael Rosen 2003
Illustrations copyright © Jonathan Langley 2003
Cover illustration copyright © Jonathan Langley 2022

ISBN: 978-0-00-712443-5

Printed and bound in the UK

OWW!

MICHAEL ROSEN
ILLUSTRATED BY JONATHAN LANGLEY

HarperCollins *Children's Books*

Piggy Piglet was wriggling in his sleep.

He wriggled,

and he jiggled,

and he rolled on to something very prickly.

OW!

This woke up Pig and all the Piglets.
"Ow!" said Piggy Piglet.
"This prickly thing hurts.
Can you help me?"

"We can bounce it off," said all the Piglets.
"We're good at bouncing."

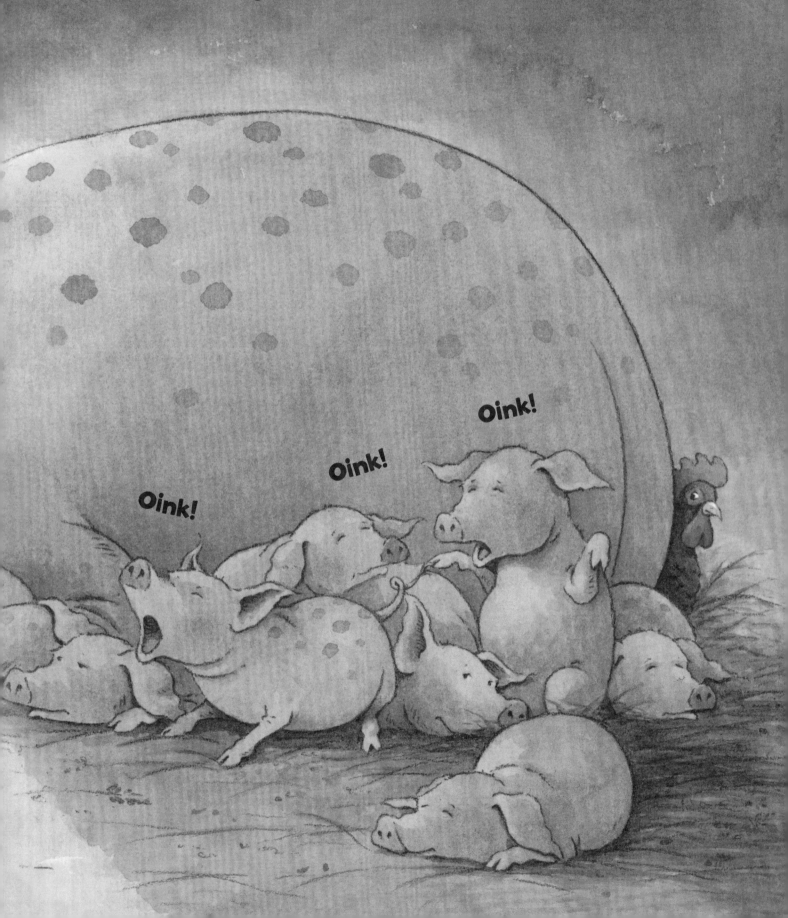

But the prickly thing prickled them.

"Let's ask Cat," said Pig and all the Piglets.
"She's the clever one." So Pig and all the Piglets
and Piggy Piglet went to find Cat.

Miaow!

"Ow!" said Piggy Piglet.
"Can you help me?"
"Easy," said Cat,
"I'll claw it off."

But the prickly thing
prickled her paw.
"Ouch!" she screeched.

Claw!

Ow!

"Try Dog," said Cat. "He's good at helping."
So Pig and all the Piglets, Cat and Piggy Piglet
went off to wake up Dog.

"Ow!" said Piggy Piglet. "Please can you help me?"

Woof!

"No problem," said Dog, "I'll whack it off."

But the prickly thing prickled his tail.

"Let's ask Cow," said Dog. "She's big and strong."

And so Pig and all the Piglets, Cat, Dog and Piggy
Piglet went off to find Cow.
"**Ow!**" said Piggy Piglet. "Please can you help me?"
"I'm sure I can push it off," said Cow.

Push!

But the prickly thing prickled her nose.
"MOO! MOO! MOO!" said Cow.
"Let's ask Sheep, she's full of ideas."

So Pig and all the Piglets, Cat, Dog, Cow and
Piggy Piglet went off to find Sheep.
"Ow!" said Piggy Piglet. "*Please* can you help me?"
"I have a plan," said Sheep. "I'll kick it off."

BAAAAA

Kick!

Oi! Oi! Oi!

But the prickly thing prickled Sheep's foot.

Ow!

"Poor Piggy Piglet," said Pig and all the Piglets,
Cat, Dog, Cow and Sheep.

"Who else can we ask?"

"How about Donkey?"

"You must be joking."

"All he thinks about is food."

"He's hungry in the morning
and hungry in the evening."

"He's even hungry
in his sleep."

But Piggy Piglet had had enough.
"I'm **SICK** of this prickly thing!
Can't ANYONE help?"

At that moment Donkey trotted up.
"EE-AW!" he said. "Any food here?"
"No!" said the animals. "We're helping Piggy Piglet."
"Well, *I* can't," said Donkey. "Too hungry."

But…but…but…

…what did Donkey see just then? Stuck on the end of Piggy Piglet's tail was something very delicious.

Ee-awww!

Donkey bent down, opened his mouth and…

...YUM!

Munch! Munch! Munch!

"Ooh, a THISTLE!" Donkey said. "I love thistles!"

And off he went.

"Yippee!" said Piggy Piglet.
"The prickly thing's GONE!"

"Well, fancy that!" said Pig and all the Piglets,
Cat, Dog, Cow and Sheep.
"I'm hungry," said Piggy Piglet.

"So are we," said the others and off they all went to get their breakfast.

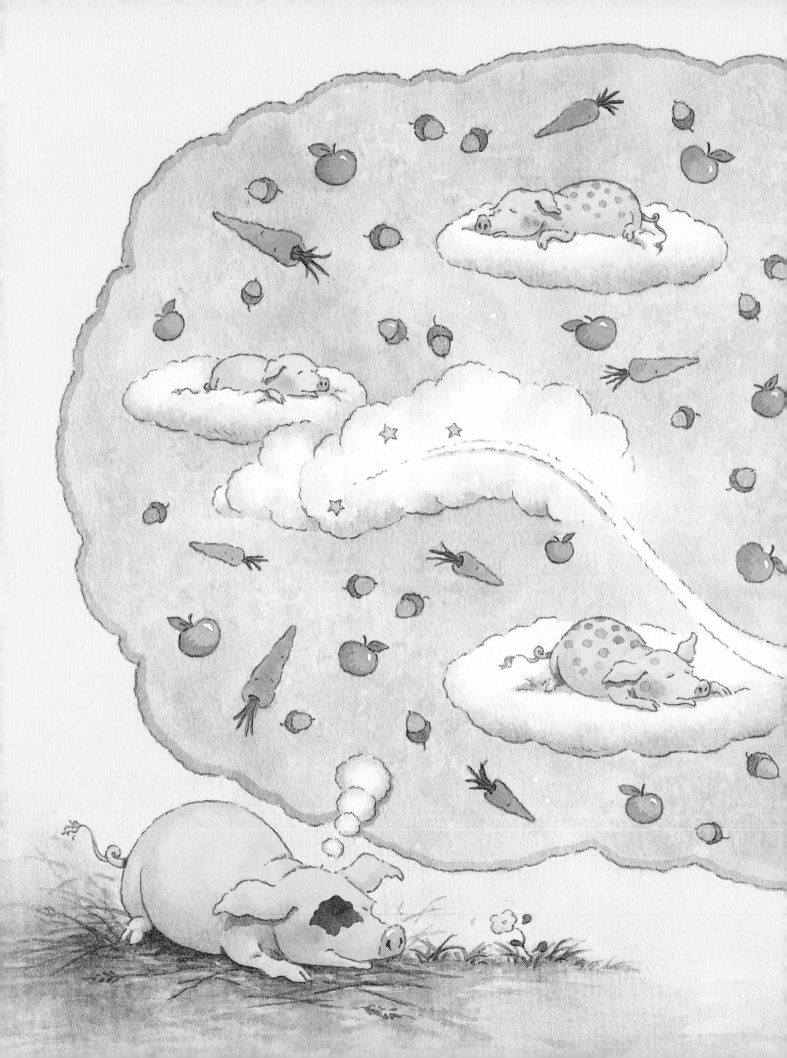

LOOK OUT FOR MORE
FUNNY FARMYARD STORIES!

FROM THE BESTSELLING AUTHOR OF *WE'RE GOING ON A BEAR HUNT*

MICHAEL ROSEN

SNORE!
A NOISY NIGHT FOR A DOZY DOG

ILLUSTRATED BY JONATHAN LANGLEY

FROM THE BESTSELLING AUTHOR OF *WE'RE GOING ON A BEAR HUNT*

MICHAEL ROSEN

SHOO!
A CRAFTY CAT WITH A CUNNING PLAN

ILLUSTRATED BY JONATHAN LANGLEY